Mandrill Mountain Math Mysteries

A STORM AT SEA

SORTING, MAPPING, AND GRIDS IN ACTION

Text by Felicia Law & Steve Way
Illustrations by Mike Spoor & David Mostyn

alphabet
soup™
an imprint of
WINDMILL BOOKS™
New York

Published in 2010 by Windmill Books, LLC
303 Park Avenue South, Suite # 1280, New York, NY 10010-3657

Adaptations to North American Edition © 2010 Windmill Books
Copyright © Diverta Ltd 2010

CREDITS: Text by Felicia Law & Steve Way, Illustrations by Mike Spoor & David Mostyn

Library of Congress Cataloging-in-Publication Data

Law, Felicia.
 A storm at sea : sorting, mapping, and grids in action / text by Felicia Law & Steve Way ; illustrations by Mike Spoor & David Mostyn. -- 1st North American ed.
     p. cm. -- (Mandrill mountain math mysteries)
 Summary: Shipwrecked on a remote island, a group of disparate monkeys try to agree on how best to survive their ordeal unaware that their actions are being watched and judged by the monkeys that rule the island.
 ISBN 978-1-60754-815-7 (library binding) -- ISBN 978-1-60754-820-1 (pbk.) -- ISBN 978-1-60754-825-6 (6-pack)
 [1. Monkeys--Fiction. 2. Shipwrecks--Fiction. 3. Survival--Fiction. 4. Mathematics--Fiction. 5. Mystery and detective stories.] I. Way, Steve. II. Spoor, Mike, ill. III. Mostyn, David, ill. IV. Title. V. Title: Sorting, mapping, and grids in action.
 PZ7.L41835Sto 2010
 [Fic]--dc22
                            2009040148

Manufactured in the United States of America

CPSIA Compliance Information: Batch #BW01W: For further information contact Windmill Books, New York, New York at 1-866-478-0556.

How it all began...

It was dark. Black storm clouds and lightning flashes swept the sky. Loud thunderclaps echoed over the sea. The noise was deafening.

Rain clattered down, whipping at the boat. Waves like mountains crashed over the deck. The boat was lifted high, then dropped sharply back into the sea.

As the boat plunged, the crate on deck started to slide. It tugged at the ropes that held it there — until they snapped.

We're going overboard.

Eek! Ouch! Hold on!

Once more the sea surged over the boat, then withdrew, dragging the crate off the deck and into the ocean. It rolled dangerously on the swell, and was carried away.

Oh no! Water is coming in!

We're sinking!

I'm scared!

Help!

Inside the crate, fingers scratched against the planks, trying to push the top off. Everyone inside was desperate to escape. And as the wood splintered, and the inhabitants glimpsed open sky, they thumped and banged even harder on their crate.

Bang it! Thump it!

The sea soaked the monkeys with cold salty water. They had to get out.

We must get out!

It's coming loose!

Quick! Shift these planks. You push and we'll pull!

Let's get Bushbaby out! She's the smallest.

- 6 -

I can see the sky now.

The monkeys scrambled out and gulped in the fresh air. A shape loomed on the horizon.

I can see land!

We'll hit that beach.

The beach was dry and warm and the monkeys were exhausted.

We made it! We made it!

At last – dry land! But was this a safe place? Their excitement and relief were mixed with nervousness. This was another land with strange trees, and who knows what else!

Howler was worried. Would the humans on the boat follow them here and snatch them again? Would they be packed in a crate once more and shipped off to some faraway place?

- 9 -

Howler looked around at the group. They couldn't have been a more mixed crowd. In fact, no two of them were the same.

You're a skinny little thing, aren't you?

And you're a big hulk — more muscle than brain if you ask me!

Hey guys, no arguing, okay?

You're beautiful. What's your name?

Why don't we all introduce ourselves? It looks like we're going to be stuck with each other for a while.

Good idea! You go first.

I'm Howler – You'll find out why soon enough.

Bushbaby

Chacma

Gibbon

Chimp

I'm Ringtail. Looks like Bushbaby, Chimp, and I are the only girls?

Mac – short for macaque

I'm Potto, a Slow Loris, but you won't find me slow when it comes to telling you what's what...

...like why are we wasting time chatting? Don't you think we should face up to what's going on here?

What do you mean?

I'm wet, cold, and tired!

We'll all be dead by tomorrow if we don't find food and water.

Potto's right.

We need to find food fast.

I don't know if there's anything I can eat here. I haven't seen any eggs yet.

Well, I need fruit. Anyone seen fruit?

What a moaner! I'm easy. Just find me a tree where I can haul myself up and sleep.

We'll starve, you'll see!

Personally, I'm happier sleeping down here.

Listen – We're all in the same situation. But if we work together as a team, we'll have a better chance of getting through.

Potto could be right. How do we know there's fresh water in this place?

Howler will have us all standing out in the rain with our mouths open.

I only eat at night. Sleep all day, eat all night.

Look, it's clear we're all different, but we've still got to work together.

Not me. Three meals a day and a good night's sleep is what I need.

Howler was beginning to understand the size of the problem. Potto's grumbling had made it clear that none of them ate the same things, slept at the same times or even in the same places. They were different shapes and sizes – with very different needs.

What was that?

What?

That noise! There's something out there. It's dangerous here. We've nowhere to hide.

We should find shelter. Who knows what danger we're in?

Quick, hide! It could be those men from the boat.

In the trees. Run!

Wait...!

Bushbaby was right! There was something out there...

From high up on the mountain, the Emperor Tamarin had watched every move the young monkeys had made.

Eight of them. Young monkeys too – and all different. There will be a lot of bickering while they figure out how to survive on this island.

He sighed deeply. It was almost certain that the young group would fail to find food and water. In time, they would starve and die. He'd seen other animals, even humans, washed up on the shores of this island, and they had all met the same fate. He doubted these small monkeys would be any different.

He lowered his eyes and closed them wearily. "How long have I been here now?" he wondered. "It must be many, many years, and in all that time, I have shared the island with Mandrill and the Hanumans, and with no one else. It would be an experience to have young monkeys around, a playful group whose chatter and mischief would break the silence of the long days..."

The Emperor sighed again. The peace of the island, and everything it stood for, must never be broken. He was both Emperor and guardian of its secrets. The Emperor, his Lord Protector, Mandrill, and the troop of loyal Hanuman soldiers would fight to the death to defend the island's secrets. "Mandrill and the Hanumans won't want those young monkeys to stay on the island one minute longer than necessary," the Emperor thought.

He opened his eyes as Mandrill entered the temple. He could tell by his flared nostrils and muscular stride, that the Lord Protector had sighted the monkeys for himself. It was obvious that Mandrill had already made up his mind.

Have you found out who they are?

No Emperor! But I'm guessing that the schooner was running illegal animals to the mainland. It's possible they got washed overboard in the storm.

The boat may come back for them, Sire, and we don't want that. Let's get rid of them now.

It would be a pity. They're young.

You can't let them stay. It will put us all in danger. And even if they're not followed here, they'll cause mayhem.

"We've been here a long time, Mandrill," the Emperor said slowly. "I often wonder what will happen when we're too old to do our sacred duties. Who will guard the island and its secrets?"

"What? You think these young monkeys have been sent here to take over? My Lord, I beg you, this is just a ragtag bunch of kids who know nothing of high destiny and service."

"My Emperor," Mandrill continued. "I see danger ahead. We must make sure they don't find the Wheel, or the Stone. And what if they start to explore the mountain and find some way to cross the ravine?"

"Stop! Stop!" interrupted the Emperor. "These young monkeys have problems that will hold them close to the shore for some time yet. There's no need for haste. First they will look for food and water and shelter. That will take them awhile. And they'll be much too frightened to move inland.

I'm not an old fool, Mandrill. I know you and the wily Hanumans will make sure these youngsters stay where you can keep an eye on them. But make sure that is all you do!"

Take it easy, Mandrill. I know you are Protector here, but I've decided to give them a chance.

I want to see what they are made of and whether they can meet the greatest challenge of all – survival.

Emperor – I strongly advise...

Enough, Mandrill! You have heard my wishes on this matter.

Then the Hanumans and I will obey your command, but...

Mandrill bowed low. There was no question that the Emperor must be obeyed, but Mandrill knew he had two jobs to do now. He must guard his Emperor with his life, as he had always done, and guard the Emperor against himself, too!

Perhaps the Emperor was getting old. Could he really believe the castaway group had some future destiny on this island?

"No," thought Mandrill. "They're just a bunch of troublemakers who will make life difficult for those of us who are dedicated to keeping this island safe! Future destiny, indeed! I'll see to it that they are a heap of dried bones on the beach before the month is out!"

But Mandrill had to think fast. He must call together the Hanumans and give them clear orders. He couldn't let the young castaways move off the beach.

I must think of cunning ways to stop them.

But first, I must set spies around the beach to report back.

Hanumans! Warrior monkeys who guard our sacred Emperor. A new threat has landed on our island...

The Hanumans gathered at once in the temple courtyard. Mandrill quickly explained the new threat and the Emperor's wishes. He warned the Hanumans that they must not let the castaway monkeys see them. The castaways should think they are alone on the island.

Mandrill told the warrior monkeys to be careful not to harm the young monkeys in any way. Their duty was to keep them fenced in, down on the beach, where they had landed. And if it proved that food and water were in short supply down there – well, so be it!

The loyalty of the Hanumans to their Emperor could not be questioned. These warrior guardians of the temple, were known for their courage and faithful service. Trained to fight with speed and stealth, they knew every detail of the island's rocky landscape, the forests that covered its slopes, and the beaches and covers that lined its shores. They knew every hiding place, every shadow, and could see through every disguise. They would carry out Mandrill's orders to the letter!

...so, while we're not going to drive these monkeys away, we're not going to help them settle here, either.

We understand you, Protector. For now we watch in secret...but later...

- 17 -

Wait everybody! Listen! We can do this if we just stick together.

We're not the first creatures to be washed up on a beach and forced to survive. There was this guy called Robinson Crusoe...

What's the point of storytelling? Right now, I want something to eat.

And somewhere to sleep.

Look! We can survive if we take a lesson from someone else's book.

This guy, Crusoe, was like us – a castaway, cold, wet, hungry, and frightened – but he survived.

How?

Robinson Crusoe's ship ran into trouble and sank. Crusoe was pitched by the waves and currents and finally tossed onto the beach of a deserted island.

Howler had caught the other castaways' attention. They were all tired, and with all the quarreling and worrying, they were ready to settle down and listen to what promised to be a good bedtime adventure story...

- 18 -

Crusoe's boat – Howler continued – went down, drowning everyone on board – for as much as Crusoe searched, he couldn't find any other survivors. He was all alone. How would he survive?

He forgot his fear when he concentrated on making himself a camp. Crusoe's first thought was to find somewhere he could curl up and sleep and feel safe.

He'd found cable and canvas from the ship, so he put up a kind of tent on the hillside and built a tall fence around it, using stakes roped together for strength.

He carefully searched the beach. Wreckage from the ship had been washed ashore.

Slowly Crusoe gathered any pieces he thought could prove useful. He found some wood, string, cloth from the sails, and some pots. But he would have to make tools to survive.

Fortunately he had a knife in his pocket, but he needed other things, like an ax for cutting down trees so he could build a table and a chair.

Eventually he made a pick-ax, a shovel, and even used strips of bark to weave himself a basket and a fishing net. He was beginning to think he might survive. But he kept his eyes and ears open. He couldn't be sure the island was deserted!

The island was in the tropics so the weather was mostly warm, but storms and heavy winds often blew in from the sea. Crusoe needed to stay warm when that happened. He needed a way to cook meat, too. Howler told the other monkeys Robinson Crusoe remembered the art of starting a fire–rubbing two sticks against each other over some dry grass.

Mac, who knew about science, joined in. "This rubbing is called friction, " he said. "It takes a long time, but eventually the rubbing heats the two pieces of wood up enough to make a spark and set the dry grass on fire!"

Howler went on with his story...

Robinson Crusoe often thought of his home and he was very lonely. But when you have to survive each day on your own work and effort, there isn't much time to think about feeling sorry for yourself.

So the days passed and Crusoe became even more skilled in the art of survival.

He planted seeds and grew food crops. He herded up wild goats, penning them where he could milk them and kill them for meat.

He found fruits and seeds and fished in the sea.

In fact, he was doing very well – until he found a footprint in the sand.

The island was visited from time to time by natives – they came there to picnic.

So he wasn't alone?

So why didn't this Crusoe talk to the visitors and escape from the island with them?

Because they were cannibals.

What's a cannibal?

Believe me, you don't want to know – but do go on Howler.

Howler went back to his story.

A few weeks before Crusoe found the footprint, he had wandered into a cove. In the cove, he found some frightening evidence that other humans might be on the island. He found bones and a skull. He also found an old fire and signs of cooking. It almost looked like evidence of a cannibal meal! This was a terrible discovery. He certainly wasn't safe if cannibals–people-eaters–visited the island!

Crusoe doubled his security. He was more watchful than ever. And then one day, a boat of native peoples came to the shore. They landed in the cove just as before, and they had a prisoner.

Crusoe had the element of surprise to help him. He was able to frighten the natives and free the prisoner. At last, the natives gave up and went back to sea.

- 22 -

Crusoe called the native Friday because that was the day on which they met.

And slowly they started to learn each other's languages and habits — and put their skills and knowledge together.

Of course, Friday knew things about the island that Crusoe didn't.

But Crusoe had done pretty well so far on his own.

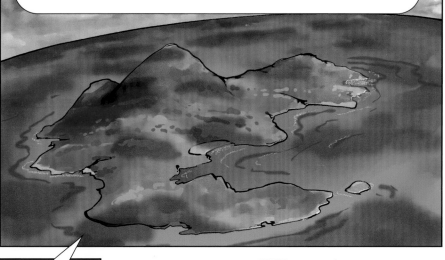

Together they explored the whole island, mapping it and finding out what was in the north, south, east, and west.

Anyhow, finally a ship arrived on the island and after a few adventures, Crusoe went on board and sailed for home.

He'd kept a calendar by carving the dates on a wooden post, which is how he knew he'd been on the island for 28 years.

28 years!

Okay guys! We may only be here for a few weeks — but who knows? Don't you think we ought to be prepared in case it's longer? All I'm saying is that we'll have a better chance if we work together.

I mean, we're all suffering from the same problems right now — we're all hungry aren't we?

You're right! Let's list the things we all eat and scavenge together. Look for everything on the list whether you eat it yourself or not.

Look — I'm pretty nifty with these thumbs. I'll weave a net like that man Crusoe did and we can use it as a larder. Store all our food in it, and sling it up in a tree so it's safe...

...from natives?

From everything! Let's get started. Work outward in a circle from here and keep each other in sight.

- 24 -

In an hour, the net was full – fruit, insects, leaves, bark – anything and everything the group could eat.

And with full stomachs – and a full store for the next day – everyone could at last relax...

and sleep...

Meanwhile, as the only nocturnal members of the group, Potto and timid Bushbaby found themselves on guard.

This was the moment the Hanumans had been waiting for. Under cover of darkness, they had crept down the mountain to to set up a challenge for the young monkeys—the first of many!

Creeping and sliding, three of them moved skillfully through the branches. Not even a twig cracked or a leaf fluttered. Each of them wore a Hanuman mask, the dark headwear that hid their bright white faces. These Sun-loving monkeys could hide more easily in the white heat of day than in the dark shadows of night. But their masks helped hide them.

Moving quietly past the sleeping youngsters, the Hanumans had no difficulty spotting the guards. Potto and Bushbaby were awake, but both were using the night hours to feed – just as every nocturnal animal did. Potto was his usual sleepy self, night or day, while Bushbaby had discovered a feast of young insects and was greedily eating her first meal of the night.

Shhh! They've set a guard on the food store...

They don't look like the fiercest of pairs!

"That's their food bag, up there on the branch," said one. "I watched a young chimp hang it there. Probably thought it was safe from prying animals."

"But he was wrong," whispered his colleague. "It's within easy reach."

"Not a bad bag, though," said the first, inspecting the carefully woven net of vines. "That chimp's got nifty fingers and we'll be wise to remember that."

"So where are we going to hide it?" asked the second Hanuman.

"Toss it in the sea," said the third member of the group. "That will get rid of it."

"No," said the first. "Mandrill said 'challenge' and that's what we'll do. We need to set up a challenge, or puzzle, that they won't have enough skills to figure out."

Mandrill's right! These monkeys have got to learn a lesson or two.

Quietly the Hanumans untied the food net and set it higher up in the tree, far higher, and coiled around a swarming wasp nest.

Right. Let's get back. Mandrill says they'll soon weaken with no food and water.

We've still got to hide the entrance to Waterfall Rock.

Yes. He doesn't want them to find the water up there.

Potto! Shh! I thought I saw shapes up in that tree. But how could I have?

Howler! Wake up, everybody! The food's gone!

How did it get up there? I slung it way down.

You thought you did, but...

The group gazed in despair at the food bag, as it swung there, high above them, protected by a swarm of angry, buzzing wasps.

Mac was suddenly quiet. This was the kind of problem his quick, intelligent brain was good at solving. The problem wasn't the bag, it was the wasps. And he knew a bit about wasps...

Guys – cut the bickering. Chimp can you do anything?

I'll get stung to pieces.

...unless the wasps are sleepy – smoke does that – it makes them drowsy.

Smoke comes from fire. Remember how Crusoe made fire?

I can try and do that. Let's get what we need.

Chimp had the thumbs for the job. Deftly twiddling the two twigs over some dry grass, she patiently worked away – until, at last, a spark caught fire.

When you hear the buzzing die down, pass me this hook to unsling the net.

The smoke from the flaming twigs drifted slowly up toward the nest. Mac had been right. The wasps reacted quickly to the smoke, leaving their nest and the food bag at its center, and fanning out in the cool night air.

Chimp's fingers were skilled in untying knots, and as the wasps buzzed more and more drowsily around her head, she deftly untied the bag and started to lower it to the ground.

From now on, she would guard it with her life!

Her arrival was greeted with a cheer. The young group had faced their first real challenge — and solved it.

They had worked together as a team, and now, the thrill of their success ran through the whole group.

We did it!

After all the excitement, it was almost dawn before the weary group was asleep once again!

But Howler couldn't sleep. Had Bushbaby been right? Were there other monkeys on this island — monkeys who wished them no good and who might even harm them?

I will have to be more cunning next time.

These monkeys must be driven off the island.

The next morning, Mandrill heard all about the young monkeys' actions and their success in rescuing their food bag. He scowled. The Hanumans had done his bidding. They had set a challenge – but, clearly, one that the young monkeys had easily solved.

So! These monkeys were going to try and match him, were they? They certainly had a few skills he hadn't banked on, but he would soon find out their weaknesses, and then, there would be no way out for them.

"Watch them even more closely," he ordered the Hanumans. "Learn who can do what and who is giving the orders. But above all, watch where they go. They mustn't move off the beach!"

But, even as Mandrill was giving these orders, the young monkeys woke up to fresh thoughts of food and water. Like Robinson Crusoe, they didn't know what the island held in store for them.

But one thing was for sure, they would need all their wits, intelligence, strength and courage to overcome the challenges that lay ahead.

Glossary

cannibals (CAN-ih-bullz) humans who eat other humans

horizon (ho-RY-zun) a line in the distance where the sky appears to meet the land or water

friction (FRIK-shun) when two things rub against each other and produce heat

macaque (muh-KAK) a very common type of monkey that is often used in animal laboratory testing

Index

C
cannibals…..22
circle…..24
crate…..4-6, 9

F
friction…..21

H
horizon…..7

M
macaque…..11
mischief…..14

S
shelter…..13, 15

T
tropics…..20

W
wasp…..27-30

For more great fiction and nonfiction go to windmillbooks.com.